Delicious English

CARAMEL TREE

www.carameltree.com

Comet Boy

CARAMEL TREE

Chapter 1

The Comet Crystals

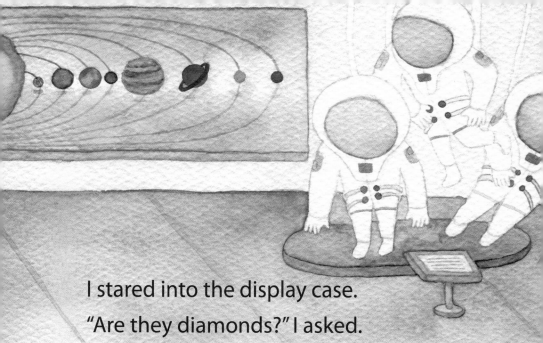

I stared into the display case.

"Are they diamonds?" I asked.

"Those are comet crystals. Everyone thinks comet pieces fall to Earth as dark rocks. That is true! But the crystals in this display are from a comet's tail," explained the Planetarium guide, Mr. Mars. That wasn't his real name. But all the staff at the Planetarium had name badges with names of planets. I thought that was cool.

Do Not Touch

I kept staring at the crystals. They seemed to be glowing.

"Can I touch them?" I asked.

"Only scientists in full bodysuits can handle them," Mr. Mars replied, as he turned to speak to Mom.

His answer made me more curious. I wondered how it would feel to touch the crystals. I pressed my fingers against the top piece of glass. Suddenly, the glass moved.

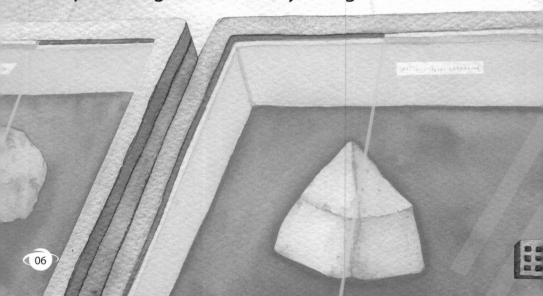

I waited for an alarm to sound. But nothing happened. The display case was not alarmed. I was surprised, but still very curious.

With no glass covering them, the comet crystals glowed even brighter. I couldn't help it. I reached in and touched the glowing crystals.

Power rushed up my arm and through my whole body. I tingled. I felt almost... *electric.*

"Gordon?" called Mom.

Uh-oh. I quickly pulled my hand out of the display case and slid the glass back into place.

'Did she see me touching the crystals?'
I wondered.

I turned around. Mom was talking to Mr.
Mars. Both of them were smiling. Luckily,
they did not see me touching the crystals.

"Let's go for lunch," Mom said.

Food! Great. I was hungry.

I ran ahead to the door and pulled the doorknob.

The huge door came right off its hinges!

Chapter 2
Rush of Power

I carefully put the huge door on the ground.

Mom was angry and worried. "The door could have fallen on my son!" she complained.

Mr. Mars was surprised and said sorry. He thought the door was loose. "Are you okay?" he asked.

"I'm fine, thanks," I said.

Mom reached across the table to feel my forehead. "You are hot. I hope you are not going to get sick," she said.

"I'm fine, Mom." I sat back.

But was I? When I pulled the doorknob, I felt a rush of power through my arm. The door came off its hinges like a paperclip.

"You are not eating," Mom fussed. "You love pizza. That *proves* you are ill."

I shook my head. "I'm not hungry, Mom. I'll wait for you in the gift shop."

I needed to be alone. I needed to think. Those crystals had done something to me. Why did I touch them?

I walked to the gift shop, being careful not to touch anything. But feeling warm like this was making me thirsty. I saw the drinking fountain and walked over to get a drink.

I was drinking water when a voice called, "Hey, you!"

It was William Ball. He was the school bully. I was surprised to see him at the Planetarium. He was the type of kid who usually went to the skate park.

"Get out of my way! I want a drink," he shouted.

I straightened up. I thought of the lunches William had stolen from me and other kids.

"You want a drink?" I asked. "Here."

I felt another rush of power. I picked up the drinking fountain and gave it to William. It was like picking up an empty bottle.

But it was filled with water. It was too heavy
for William. He dropped it on his feet. You
should have seen the look on William's face!
No more skating around for him for a while!

Chapter 3
A Robbery

William screamed like a baby. His screams echoed through the Planetarium. I quietly walked over to the book section in the gift shop and picked up a book on comets. I needed to learn about them. Fast!

I read about a comet that crashed into one of Jupiter's oceans. *Pffft!* That was the end of the comet. It lost all its power after falling into the ocean.

Mom was happy to see me reading a book. "Strange about William Ball," Mom said as we walked to the cashier.

I hid a smile. "Maybe next time he will decide to drink from a glass."

Just then, outside the Planetarium, an alarm rang.

Everyone ran to the window.

A masked man ran out of the jewelry store across the street. He was carrying a suitcase with diamonds spilling out the top.

People started screaming. "A robbery! Where are the police?"

The robber ran toward a blue car parked nearby. An old woman leaning on a cane stood in his way. He pushed her to the ground.

I was growing even hotter than before. I didn't like the man being rough on an old lady. Before I knew what I was doing, I ran across the street.

I reached the car as the robber started the engine.

"Get out of my way, kid – or I'll run you over," threatened the robber.

"You should pick on someone your own size," I shouted.

I lifted the car and turned it over.

Chapter 4
One Chance

Mr. Mars

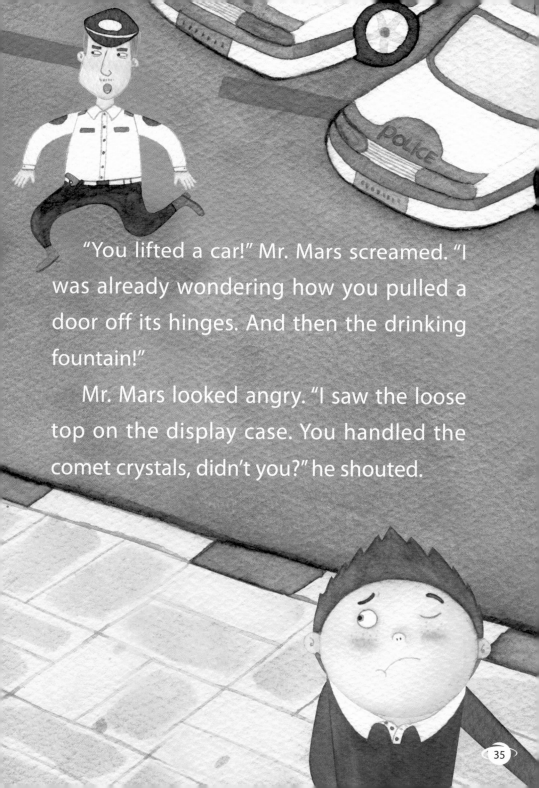

"You lifted a car!" Mr. Mars screamed. "I was already wondering how you pulled a door off its hinges. And then the drinking fountain!"

Mr. Mars looked angry. "I saw the loose top on the display case. You handled the comet crystals, didn't you?" he shouted.

Mom stepped between us. "Now just a minute. There's no need to shout at my son."

Mr. Mars gave a thin smile. "You're right. This isn't the time for shouting. But it is the time for Gordon to be checked by a team of scientists. Look at him! He's *glowing!*"

Mr. Mars was wearing big thick gloves. He reached out to grab me. Three more Planetarium staff were behind him. They were wearing full bodysuits. Oh no! This looked bad. I did not want to be taken to a science lab.

I started running.

"You come back here!" Mr. Mars
screamed.

He was chasing me with the three
staff in full bodysuits close behind.

I kept running. I zoomed way ahead
of them. I was running faster than I ever
thought I could.

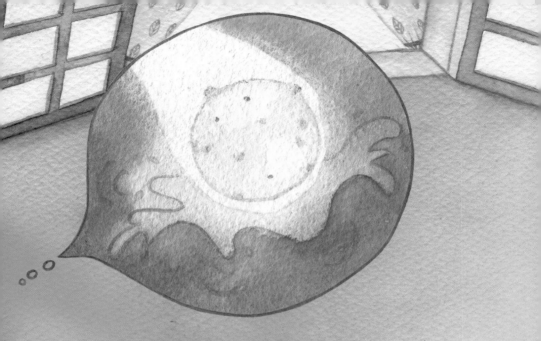

Then I remembered the comet that crashed into an ocean on Jupiter. *Pffft!* It lost all its power in the water.

I had one chance. I had to get into water. That was the only way to lose the power of the comet crystals.

I ran around the block toward the swimming pool. I could hear Mr. Mars screaming behind me. "You stop right there!"

I got to the swimming pool ahead of Mr. Mars. Other people in bathing suits stared at me.

I jumped into the pool with all my clothes on. Splash!

Down, down, I sank…

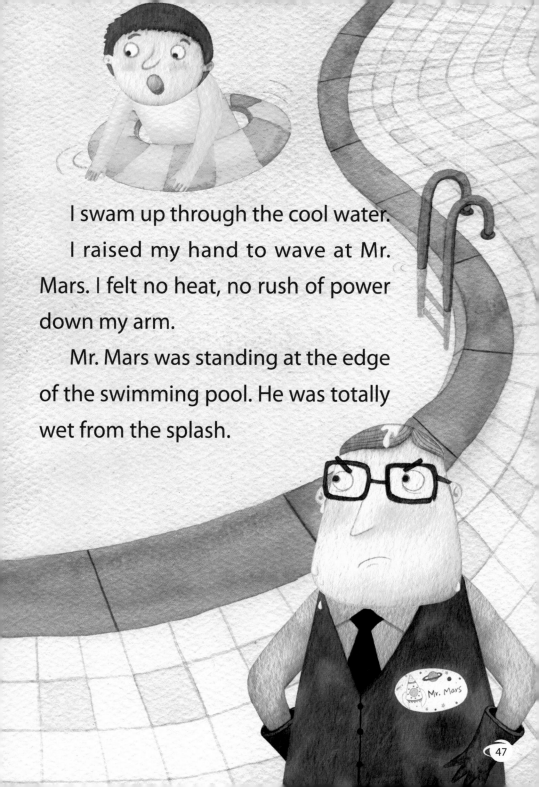

I swam up through the cool water.

I raised my hand to wave at Mr. Mars. I felt no heat, no rush of power down my arm.

Mr. Mars was standing at the edge of the swimming pool. He was totally wet from the splash.

"Just what are you up to, young man?"
asked Mr. Mars.

I grinned back at him. "*Pffft!*" I said.